The Blue Eyes Trilogy

Jason Poncio

Three Novels by Jason Poncio

The Trilogy Collection

Book One: Blue Eyes

Book Two: Forever Love

Book Three: Hunt Down

BLUE EYES

By Jason Poncio

COPYRIGHT PAGE

The first time Jason saw her, the air smelled like fallen leaves and polished wood.

The school auditorium always carried that scent in autumn dust warmed by stage lights, varnish rubbed thin by decades of performances, paper programs still crisp and faintly sweet with ink. Parents filled the rows with nervous chatter, coats brushing, voices overlapping like static. The room hummed with expectation.

Jason sat in the second row with the choir, fifteen years old and trying not to disappear.

He had learned early how to be present without being seen. How to take up as little space as possible. Music was the one place he didn't feel invisible, the one place his voice mattered even if his body didn't. Still, that night, he felt smaller than usual, folded into himself as the lights dimmed.

Then she walked out.

She didn't pause. She didn't perform her entrance. She simply stepped beneath the lights as if they had been waiting for her all along. Not because she demanded attention, but because it found her naturally.

Her hair fell just past her shoulders, brown and soft, catching the glow as she moved. When she smiled at the crowd, something inside Jason shifted quietly, irreversibly.

But it was her eyes that held him.

Blue.

Not sharp. Not dazzling. Not the kind of blue that stole focus.

The kind that stayed.

They didn't search the room or dart from face to face. They rested, calm and steady, like water that didn't need to prove its depth. The kind of blue that felt safe, even from a distance.

Something in Jason tuned itself to that color and never quite untuned again.

She sang.

Her voice wasn't loud. It didn't push. It wrapped around the room with warmth instead of force, confidence without strain. It felt intentional, intimate, as if she were singing to people rather than at them.

Jason forgot his own entrance twice. He caught himself staring, not thinking in words but feeling something deeper than language a recognition without logic.

He didn't know her name yet.

But somehow, he trusted her.

She was seventeen. A junior. Old enough to move through the world with a quiet confidence that didn't need validation. During rehearsals, she flipped pages calmly, adjusted her music folder without fuss, helped others without announcing it.

They met properly a week later.

Jason was sorting sheet music when a shadow fell across the stand beside him.

"You're a tenor, right?" she asked.

He looked up and nearly forgot how to breathe.

Her eyes were bluer up close clearer somehow, softer. Not overwhelming. Just present.

"Yeah," he said, nodding too fast.

"I'm Blue," she said. "If you ever get lost, just watch me. I cue early."

It wasn't flirtation.

It wasn't dramatic.

It was kindness.

And it wrecked him.

From that moment on, she became a constant not loudly, not obviously, but steadily. She noticed when he was unsure, stepped in when others didn't, protected him without making him feel small.

When older students teased him for being younger, she shut it down with a look that needed no explanation. When he doubted his voice, she encouraged him without exaggeration.

"You've got something," she told him once during a break, leaning against the piano. "You just don't know it yet."

Jason carried those words like armor.

He didn't tell her how close he stood just to feel her presence. How her laugh replayed in his head at night. How her eyes felt like a place he could rest without explanation.

She never looked at him the way he looked at her.

She saw a younger friend. A talented kid. Someone worth protecting.

And Jason loved her too much to complicate her world.

Time moved the way it always does without permission.

Graduation arrived in a blur of sunlight and applause. Blue crossed the field in her cap and gown, calm as ever, her smile steady. Jason clapped harder than anyone, pride tangled with something heavier he didn't yet have a name for.

They hugged goodbye.

It was brief. Innocent. A moment that felt too small for how much it meant.

"Don't stop singing," she said.

"I won't," he promised.

They meant it when they said they'd keep in touch.

Life didn't.

Without her, the halls felt emptier. The music room echoed differently. Jason poured himself into songwriting lyrics he didn't fully understand yet, about distance and longing and something unnamed that lived behind memory.

At night, he lay on his bed listening to the radio, the clock glowing softly in the dark. Love songs sounded different now less like fantasy, more like confession.

One night, he wrote a song.

He didn't use her name.

He didn't need to.

Every note knew exactly who it was for.

Recording it made his hands shake. Listening back, he felt exposed, as if he'd finally said everything he never said out loud. It scared him and freed him.

The song found people.

It found ears, then hearts. People asked what inspired it.

"A feeling," he'd say.

"A moment that stayed."

Inside, it was always her.

Jason grew up.

He chased music, then stability, then a version of success that looked good from the outside. He learned how to survive rooms, how to adapt, how to harden just enough without losing himself.

Love came and went. Some was good. Some cut deep. He married, believing in the structure of commitment even when he didn't fully understand himself yet. He tried to build a life that made sense on paper.

But there were quiet nights unguarded nights when he thought of Blue.

He wondered if her eyes were still the same. If she ever remembered the kid who watched her cue early.

The marriage ended without fireworks. Just exhaustion. Understanding. Pain carried quietly. Divorce stripped him raw, forced him to sit with himself without distraction.

Late one night, scrolling through old contacts, he saw her name.

Blue.

His heart stuttered.

He stared at the screen longer than he should have.

Then he typed.

Hey. Long time. I hope you're doing well.

He almost didn't send it.

She replied the next morning.

Jason. I was just thinking about you.

Something shifted subtle but undeniable. Like a door opening that had never fully closed.

They talked like no time had passed.

Surface updates turned into laughter. Laughter turned into honesty. They spoke of mistakes without defensiveness, growth without ego. They shared the parts of themselves they'd earned through loss.

Blue was still kind. Still steady. Still calm but shaped now by life lived fully. Her strength felt deeper, quieter.

When they met again in person, Jason noticed it immediately.

Her eyes.

Still blue.

Still endless.

Sitting across from her in a quiet café, he felt fifteen again but this time, he didn't feel small.

"I never told you something," he said.

She listened.

She always had.

He told her everything how he adored her, how the song was about her, how her kindness changed the way he saw himself. How her presence taught him what steady love looked like before he even knew what love was.

She didn't interrupt.

When he finished, her eyes were glassy but warm.

"I didn't know," she said softly. "But I feel it now."

What formed between them wasn't rushed.

It wasn't loud.

It was honest.

They didn't promise forever.

They didn't define it.

They chose presence.

They walked side by side not ahead, not behind. Music still lived in Jason. Blue still grounded him.

The past no longer hurt.

It informed.

Every wrong turn had led him here.

One night, she asked, "Do you regret not telling me sooner?"

Jason smiled.

"No," he said. "We wouldn't be who we are now."

Some stories aren't meant to burn bright and fast.

Some are meant to glow slowly over a lifetime.

Blue eyes don't always mean youth or longing.

Sometimes they mean clarity.

And some things the most important things are meant to take the long way home

About the Author

Jason Poncio is a writer and musician whose work explores timing, memory, and the quiet moments that shape a life. He writes across formats, including scripted storytelling, fiction, and music, often blending emotional restraint with lived experience.

His scripts and stories focus on character-driven narratives, while his songwriting serves as an extension of the same voice reflective, honest, and grounded. Whether on the page or in music, Jason's work centers on connection, growth, and the stories that stay with us long after the moment has passed.

Blue Eyes reflects his belief that some stories aren't meant to rush, but to unfold over time.

FOREVER LOVE

A Sequel to Blue Eyes

By Jason Poncio

COPYRIGHT PAGE

The Name of It

Forever love isn't loud.

It doesn't announce itself or demand belief.

It simply stays.

I feel it most when the world is quiet when the noise fades
and I'm left alone with memory. That's when her name
settles into my chest like it always has. Not heavy. Not sharp.
Just... there. Permanent.

I've loved before. But this was different. This was something
God-written, not man-made.

Blue Eyes, Again

They never left me.

Those blue eyes clear enough to drown in, strong enough to survive storms. They followed me through songs, through pages, through scripts that never needed her name written because she lived between every line.

She doesn't believe she deserves that kind of love.

But love doesn't ask permission.

And God doesn't bless out of fairness He blesses out of purpose.

What Was Given

Some people come into your life to teach you.

Some come to test you.

And some... some come to stay, even when they're gone.

She was given to me not as a moment, but as a truth. A
reminder that real connection doesn't fade it waits.

The Wait

Waiting isn't passive.

It's not weakness.

Waiting is waking up every day and choosing not to run.

It's hearing every logical reason to walk away and feeling something deeper say, Not yet.

The signs weren't loud. They never are.

They came as stillness. As resistance. As doors that refused to close.

Doubt

There were days I questioned everything.

Days I told myself love was a story people tell when they're afraid to be alone.

"Do I still believe in love?" I asked the silence.

And the silence answered with her.

I don't believe in love as an idea.

I believe in her.

Memory

I remember holding her.

The way time slowed like it respected us.

The way her body fit into my arms as if it had been waiting its whole life to land there.

Those blue eyes.

Those lips soft, confident, dangerous in how easily they made me forget the rest of the world.

When I love, I LOVE.

And that kind of love is sacred.

Sacred Things

Sacred doesn't mean perfect.

It means chosen.

It means vulnerable.

It means laying it all on the line with nothing but faith and truth between two people.

What we had was rare not because it was easy, but because it was real.

The Wilderness

Now I walk the wilderness.

Not lost just alone.

Not broken just quiet.

I pour myself into work, into creation, into being the father
my son deserves. I build. I focus. I grow.

Solitude isn't punishment.

It's preparation.

Fatherhood

My son grounds me.

He reminds me what love looks like when it's fearless and honest.

He doesn't question whether he's worthy.

He simply receives.

I learn from him every day.

Distance

Distance doesn't erase truth.

It clarifies it.

I don't chase.

I don't beg.

I trust what was planted will grow when it's ready.

Her Fear

I know her fear.

I felt it the moment she looked away instead of leaning in.

Fear wears many disguises logic, timing, self-doubt.

But fear has one weakness: it can't survive love forever.

What I Know

I know what intimacy really means.

It's not bodies it's exposure.

When two people lay their souls bare, they don't forget each other. Ever.

That kind of connection doesn't expire.

Time

Time is misunderstood.

It doesn't heal everything.

It reveals.

And what time keeps bringing back to me... is her.

The Question

Will fear win?

Or will love conquer all?

Every great story hangs on that question.

The Road

No road is easy.

Anyone who promises easy is lying.

But a road with me?

It would be full of laughter, depth, late nights, wild ideas, and an energy that doesn't fade.

Love that builds.

Love that protects.

Love that shows up.

Patience

Patience is strength disguised as stillness.

I wait not because I'm unsure,

but because I'm certain enough not to force what must be chosen freely.

God's Hand

I've learned that when God is involved, delay isn't denial.

Sometimes He waits until both hearts are ready to recognize the miracle they're standing in.

Creation

Every song I write carries her echo.

Every page I fill knows her rhythm.

She lives in the art because she lived in the truth first.

If She Knew

If she knew how deeply she changed me...

how she raised my standard, my faith, my capacity to love

she might finally understand she was never too much.

She was exactly enough.

Still Here

I'm still here.

Not frozen.

Not stuck.

Just faithful to something real.

Love Redefined

Love isn't possession.

It's presence.

Even in absence.

The Invitation

If she ever chooses to step forward

not in fear, not in doubt, but in truth.

She'll find I never left.

Forever

Forever isn't a promise you make out loud.

It's the quiet decision you make every day not to let go of what God placed in your care.

Blue Eyes, Forever

Blue Eyes was the beginning.

Forever Love is the becoming.

Not a fantasy.

A testimony.

The Last Line

Some loves don't fade.

They wait.

And when the time comes

they change everything.

Page 26 The Moment Love Chose Us

I didn't hear her arrive.

I felt her.

Some connections announce themselves without sound like a change in air pressure, like a familiar warmth returning to a room that's been cold for too long. I looked up, and there she was.

The same blue eyes.

Older now. Braver. Still dangerous in the way they saw straight through me.

For a second, neither of us moved.

Time didn't stop it bowed.

"I didn't know if you'd still be here," she said, her voice steady but her hands giving her away.

"I told you," I answered quietly. "I don't leave things that matter."

She swallowed. The silence between us carried years questions, prayers, restraint, growth. Not distance... preparation.

"I was afraid," she said. Not as an excuse. As a truth.

"I know," I replied. "Fear's loud. Love's patient."

She stepped closer, and I could see it in her eyes the war she'd fought inside herself. The realization that safety isn't found in running, but in standing still with the right person.

"I didn't think I deserved you," she whispered.

I shook my head, just once.

"This was never about deserve. It was about need. About timing. About God knowing what we couldn't see yet."

Her breath caught. Mine did too.

When I pulled her into my arms, it wasn't desperate. It wasn't rushed. It was familiar like coming home after a long road and realizing the door had never been locked.

She fit. She always had.

Her head rested against my chest, and I felt the exhale she'd been holding for years. The kind of release that only comes when truth finally outweighs fear.

"I'm here," she said.

"So am I."

I tilted her chin up, met those blue eyes again eyes that had inspired songs, pages, silence, faith. I didn't rush the kiss. I let it arrive when it was ready.

It was soft. Certain. Sacred.

Not the spark of a beginning

the flame of something that survived.

Love didn't conquer fear by force.

It outlasted it.

And in that moment, I knew:

Some stories don't end when the chapter closes.

They begin

when both hearts finally say yes.

About the Author

Jason Poncio is a writer and musician whose work explores timing, memory, and the quiet moments that shape a life. He writes across formats, including scripted storytelling, fiction, and music, often blending emotional restraint with lived experience.

His scripts and stories focus on character-driven narratives, while his songwriting serves as an extension of the same voice reflective, honest, and grounded. Whether on the page or in music, Jason's work centers on connection, growth, and the stories that stay with us long after the moment has passed.

Forever Love reflects his belief that some stories aren't meant to rush, but to unfold over time.

HUNT DOWN

Written by
Jason Poncio

Copyright Page

Copyright © 2026 by **Jimmy Star Entertainment**
All rights reserved.

No part of this book may be reproduced, distributed, transmitted, or stored in any form or by any means—electronic, mechanical, photocopying, recording, or otherwise—without prior written permission from the publisher, except for brief quotations used in reviews or scholarly works.

This is a work of fiction. Names, characters, places, and events are either the product of the author's imagination or used fictitiously. Any resemblance to actual persons, living or dead, events, or locations is purely coincidental.

Published by
Jimmy Star Entertainment

First Edition

Table of Contents

Chapter 1 — Saturday Code
Chapter 2 — The Edge of the Course
Chapter 3 — Team Split
Chapter 4 — The Head Start
Chapter 5 — Sound Carries
Chapter 6 — First Tag
Chapter 7 — Moonlight Rules
Chapter 8 — False Signal
Chapter 9 — The Woods Breathe
Chapter 10 — The Clearing
Chapter 11 — The Lone Runner
Chapter 12 — The Creek Line
Chapter 13 — Two Left
Chapter 14 — The Howl
Chapter 15 — Fear Changes Movement
Chapter 16 — Final Chase
Chapter 17 — No One Calls It
Chapter 18 — The Watcher Feeling
Chapter 19 — Exit Rule
Chapter 20 — Edge of Neighborhood
Chapter 21 — The Tradition
Chapter 22 — The Hunt Never Ends

HUNT DOWN

Chapter 1 — Saturday Code

No texts.
No group chat.
No adults knew.

If you knew, you knew.

Saturday nights meant one thing: the Hunt.

By sunset, bikes were ditched behind Jason's fence.
Flashlights checked. Shoes double-knotted. Twelve of them.
Every time. No substitutes.

Jason didn't call himself leader.
Everyone followed him anyway.

The rule was simple:

Two teams.
Acres of golf course.
Woods on three sides.
Moon above.

Run—or be hu

Chapter 2 — The Edge of the Course

The golf course looked normal in daylight—trimmed greens, white flags, sand traps like sleeping scars.

At night it turned into something else.

Shadows stretched wrong. Trees leaned closer. Sounds traveled too far.

The woods wrapped around the fairways like a waiting audience.

Jason raised his hand.

"Tonight—full perimeter allowed."

A few nervous laughs.

That meant deep woods were in play

Chapter 3 — Team Split

They split into two groups of six.

Hunters and Ghosts.

Ghosts got a five-minute head start. Hunters tracked, tagged, and eliminated.

No hiding longer than ten minutes.
No climbing trees.
No leaving the boundary creek.

Jason always hunted.

Not because he liked chasing.

Because he liked finding

Chapter 4 — The Head Start

The Ghosts took off—sprinting across the open fairway before vanishing into tree shadow.

Branches snapped. Grass hissed.

Then silence.

The moon rose higher—round and pale—painting everything silver.

Jason started counting.

Slow.
Calm.
Intentional.

When he hit sixty, he smiled.

"The hunt is on."

Chapter 5 — Sound Carries

At night, sound lies.

Footsteps feel closer. Whispers travel sideways.

Jason signaled two flankers. No yelling—only hand signs now.

They moved low and fast through rough grass.

A distant laugh echoed.

"Decoy," Jason whispered.

They kept moving.

Chapter 6 — First Tag

Movement near the sand trap.

A runner broke left—too fast, too loud.

Jason cut angle instead of distance.

Intercepted.

Tag.

"Dead," Jason said quietly.

The runner groaned. "Already?!"

"Too straight," Jason said. "You ran straight."

Chapter 7 — Moonlight Rules

Clouds shifted.

The full moon lit the open green like a spotlight.

Nobody crossed open ground now—only edges and shadows.

That was Jason's rule:

Moonlight exposes the careless.

From the treeline came a whistle—their distress signal.

Someone was surrounded.

Chapter 8 — False Signal

They rushed—then Jason slowed.

"Wait."

No follow-up whistle.

Trap.

Two Ghosts burst from brush behind them.

One tagged a Hunter before anyone reacted.

Chaos.
Running.
Shouting.
Laughter.

Then stillness again

Chapter 9 — The Woods Breathe

Deeper now.

The woods changed the air—colder, heavier.

One whispered, "Feels like we're not alone tonight."

Jason didn't answer.

Because he felt it too.

Not watched.

Not hunted.

Noticed.

Chapter 10 — The Clearing

They reached the old maintenance clearing—unused shed, rusted mower, broken fence.

Perfect ambush ground.

Jason circled wide instead of entering.

Two Ghosts hiding inside were caught from behind.

"Unfair!" one yelled.

"Predictable," Jason replied.

Chapter 11 — The Lone Runner

Only three Ghosts remained.

One ran solo—fast, disciplined.

Jason tracked sign: bent grass, broken stems.

"Whoever this is—he thinks," Jason said.

Then he smiled.

"Good."

Chapter 12 — The Creek Line

The boundary creek shimmered under moonlight.

Footprints stopped at the bank.

No crossing allowed.

So where did he go?

Jason looked up.

Mud on a low branch.

"He doubled back overhead."

The tag came seconds later.

Respect earned.

Chapter 13 — Two Left

The last two Ghosts stayed together.

Smart.

Pairs survive longer.

But pairs also make more noise.

Jason split his Hunters into silent wedges.

Pressure from both sides.

No escape route

Chapter 14 — The Howl

Then it came.

A real sound.

Not a kid.
Not a joke.

A distant howl from deep woods.

Everyone froze.

"Coyotes?" someone whispered.

Jason listened.

"Maybe," he said.

But he wasn't convinced.

Chapter 15 — Fear Changes Movement

After that, everyone moved differently.

Faster.
Closer.

No more cocky laughter.

The game shifted—from fun to primal.

Hunter and hunted blurred.

Chapter 16 — Final Chase

The last Ghost bolted across open green.

Desperate.

Moonlight caught him fully exposed.

Jason sprinted.

Grass tore underfoot.
Breath burned.

Tag.

Game over.

Chapter 17 — No One Calls It

But nobody celebrated.

The woods were too quiet.

No insects.
No wind.

One whispered, "Do you feel that?"

Everyone did.

Chapter 18 — The Watcher Feeling

They gathered center field.

Backs inward. Eyes outward.

That ancient instinct crawled up their spines.

Being watched.

Jason scanned the treeline.

Nothing moved.

Which made it worse.

Chapter 19 — Exit Rule

Jason clapped once.

"Game done. Group exit."

Nobody argued.

They left together—tight formation.

Flashlights off.

Moonlight only.

Chapter 20 — Edge of Neighborhood

Streetlights appeared.

Normal sound returned.

Crickets.
TV noise.
A car door slamming.

Reality resumed.

Everyone laughed—louder than necessary.

Chapter 21 — The Tradition

They kept playing every Saturday.

Same rules.
Same teams.
Same moon when they could get it.

Nobody talked about the howl again.

Nobody forgot it either.

Chapter 22 — The Hunt Never Ends

Years later, Jason would still remember those nights.

The chase.
The brotherhood.
The edge between game and something older.

Because some hunts are more than games.

Some hunts train you to lead.
To track.
To protect your people.

And once you've led the hunt—

You never really stop.

The Hunt is always on.

Dedication

For the kids who learned early
that games teach you things
you won't understand
until much later.

And for the ones
who always heard something
in the woods
that no one else wanted to name

About the Author

Jason Poncio writes stories rooted in memory, instinct, and the thin line between play and survival. His work explores leadership learned before adulthood, the unspoken rules of belonging, and the moments when ordinary places turn quietly dangerous after dark.

Drawn to minimalism and tension, Poncio favors clean language, sharp pacing, and emotional restraint—allowing atmosphere and implication to do the heavy lifting. His stories often feel less like fiction and more like something remembered a little too clearly.

HUNT DOWN is his meditation on boyhood ritual, the origins of leadership, and the hunts that never really end.